LOONIVERSE

DINOSAUR DISASTER

BY DAVID LUBAR

ILLUSTRATED BY

MATT LOVERIDGE

SCHOLASTIC INC.

Read all the

LOONIVERSE books!

#2

table of contents

FOR FRANK, HEATHER, VAUGHN, AND HOLDEN SCHAFFER, FAR AWAY BUT NEAR AT HEART.—DL

Library of Congress Cataloging-in-Publication Data
Lubar, David.
Dinosaur disaster / written by David Lubar ; illustrated by Matt Loveridge.
pages cm — (Looniverse ; 3)
Summary: Ed, his friends, and even his little sister are eager to go to Dinosaur Discovery, but ever since he found the magic coin called Silver Center, strange things happen around Ed—so he is not surprised to find that a blue dinosaur has followed his sister home.
ISBN 978-0-545-49605-6 (hardcover) — ISBN 978-0-545-49606-3 (pbk.)
1. Dinosaurs—Juvenile fiction. 2. Coins—Juvenile fiction. 3. Magic—Juvenile fiction. 4. Brothers and sisters—Juvenile fiction. [1. Dinosaurs—Fiction. 2. Coins—Fiction. 3. Magic—Fiction. 4. Brothers and sisters—Fiction.]
I. Loveridge, Matt, illustrator. II. Title.
PZ7.L96775Din 2013
813.54--dc23
2013011699

ISBN 978-0-545-49605-6 (hardcover) / ISBN 978-0-545-49606-3 (paperback)

12 11 10 9 8 7 6 5 4 3 2 13 14 15 16 17 18/0

Printed in China 38
First Scholastic printing, November 2013

Illustrated by Matt Loveridge
Book design by Liz Herzog

chapter 1

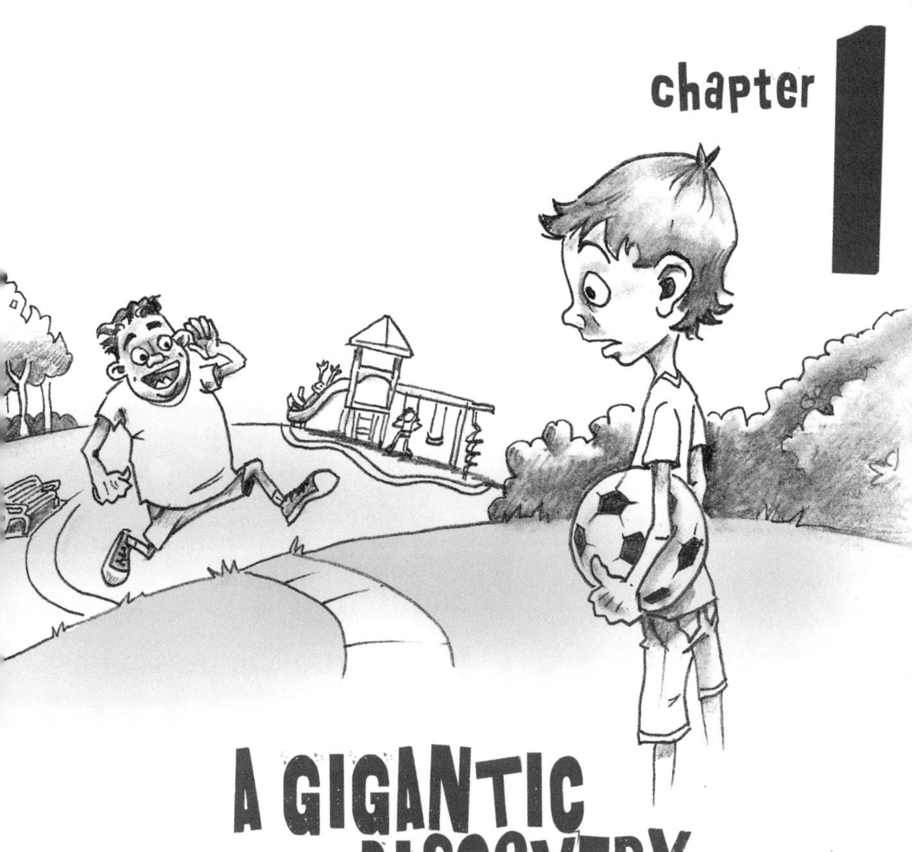

A GIGANTIC DISCOVERY

"Dinosaurs!" my friend Moose screamed as he ran toward me. "Dinosaurs! Dinosaurs! *Diiiiiinosaurssss!*"

The word got louder as he got closer.

"Dinosaurs? Where?" I asked. I didn't see any thundering lizards chasing him.

I'd just reached the town park. We were meeting there to kick around my soccer ball.

"This way, Ed," Moose said. He grabbed my arm and raced down the street."

"Real live dinosaurs?" I asked as I touched the magic coin in my pocket. I know that might sound like a crazy question, but after I found the Silver Center, I became the Stranger. Now I have the power to make strange things happen. For example, when I said, **"MONEY DOESN'T GROW ON TREES,"** my little brother, Derwin, decided it had to grow somewhere. So he looked under trees — and he found money there! Lots of other strange things happened, too. The problem is, I don't know how to control my power. I wondered whether I'd accidentally said something that would make dinosaurs appear.

"They're almost real," Moose said. A block later, he stopped running and pointed at a sign. "Look! See?"

I looked. I saw.

"We *have* to go to that," I said.

"For sure," Moose said.

Just then, our friend Quentin One rode up. "Are you guys going to this?" he asked.

"Absolutely," I said.

"I'm going tomorrow," Quentin said as he pedaled away. "They're giving out dinosaur bobbleheads to the first hundred people."

"Bobbleheads?!" I shouted. I LOVED bobbleheads. I had football and baseball players, but no dinosaurs.

"We have to get there early tomorrow," I told Moose. "I need to go ask my parents *right now*." I figured the sooner I asked, the better my chances were.

"Me, too," Moose said. He raced toward his house.

"Moose!" I yelled.

"What?" he asked.

"You can let go of my arm now," I said.

"Oops, sorry," he said as he released me.

I understood. I was excited, too. When I got home, I found Mom in the living room, reading a book about our solar system. That was a good sign. Mom liked science. There was no way she'd say no to Dinosaur Discovery.

Before I could open my mouth, Mom said something worse than "no." "Oh, good. There you are. I'll need your help tomorrow morning. So don't make any plans."

Tomorrow morning!? I felt as if someone had snatched a bobblehead from my hands, slammed it to the floor, and stomped it into tiny pieces.

chapter 2

A PERFECT PLAN

"What do you need me to do?" I asked Mom.

"Even though it's Saturday, your father and I both have to work tomorrow," she said. "Your sister Sarah Beth is old enough to watch Derwin and Libby, but I want you around in case she needs help."

I opened my mouth to argue. But then I smiled. A solution had popped up in my mind.

"I have an idea," I said. "Sarah Beth and I could take them to this educational show."

"What show?" Mom asked.

"It's all about dinosaurs," I said. "It's very scientific." I held my breath and waited. Sometimes, Mom was not thrilled about things that were loud, large, and dangerous. Naturally, I was hoping Dinosaur Discovery would be all three of those things.

Mom smiled. "That's a wonderful idea, Ed," she said.

"So can we go tomorrow?" I asked.

"Sure," Mom said. "I'll drop you all off on the way to work."

"Great." I rushed off to give Moose the good news.

“My folks told me I can go,” Moose said. “Mouse wants to come, too.”

“THE MORE, THE MERRIER,” I said. Mouse was Moose’s older brother.

As I hung up the phone, I noticed Derwin behind me. “Hey, you just gave me a great idea,” he said. He ran off to his room.

I followed him. He gathered all his toy soldiers that were scattered across the floor and tossed them in a box. “You’re right,” he said. “They’re merrier.”

The soldiers had changed poses. They looked like they were enjoying themselves.

I was so used to Derwin doing things like this around me now that I was the Stranger, I didn't even blink. "We're seeing dinosaurs tomorrow," I told him.

"Yay!" he screamed.

I told Sarah Beth next.

She had to write a report on dinosaurs for school, so she agreed Dinosaur Discovery would be worth seeing. *Two down, one to go,* I thought.

I found Libby, my little sister, in the kitchen.

"Guess what?" I said.

"What?" she asked.

"We're going to see dinosaurs — gigantic dinosaurs that move, eat, and make loud noises. Isn't that awesome?"

Her eyes widened. Her jaw dropped. Then she made a loud noise.

I stood there, stunned, as Libby raced out of the kitchen. She ran up the stairs, dived into her room, and slammed her door shut.

As I headed after her, one thought filled my mind: *How can I keep her from ruining my plans?*

Chapter 3

It's a Deal

I knocked on Libby's door. She didn't answer, so I peeked inside.

"What's wrong?" I asked as I walked in.

"I don't like dinosaurs," she said.

"Why?" I asked. I couldn't imagine anyone feeling that way.

"They're big," she said.

"I'm big," I said, standing on my tiptoes and leaning over her bed. "And you aren't scared of me."

"You don't roar," she said. "And you read stories to me."

I noticed she'd loosened her grip on her animals. I let out a roar. Libby giggled. I let out a louder roar.

"I really want to see the dinosaurs," I said. "Please come. If you get scared, we can go back home."

"Well . . . okay," she said.

"Great," I said.

"If . . ." she added.

"If what?" I asked.

"If you read me a bedtime story tonight," she said.

I paused. Right after I'd found the Silver Center, I'd read Libby a bedtime story about the Pied Piper and the rats. The next morning, thanks to my power and her imagination, the living room was filled with mice.

Reading Libby another story could mean trouble. But I really wanted that bobblehead. So, I'd just have to find a safe story.

"Okay," I said. "It's a deal. Story tonight, dinosaurs tomorrow."

That night, I looked for a book that wouldn't cause any problems.

I picked *The Bluebird Who Followed Me Home.* I figured that if a real bluebird ever followed Libby home, it would be one small bird, not a whole roomful of mice. And even if the bird made a mess and I got stuck cleaning it up, how much poop would one bluebird poop? Not much, I imagined.

I started reading. Libby was asleep by the time I finished. I tiptoed out of her room.

“Dinosaurs,” I said as I climbed into bed. I thought about all the amazing things I would see and do tomorrow. I had a feeling it was going to be an unforgettable day.

chapter 4

SHOWTIME

At breakfast, I gulped my cereal down so fast, I almost swallowed my spoon. “All right,” I said. “Let’s go see those dinosaurs.”

Derwin and Libby looked up at me from their full bowls. I wanted to scream. But I knew that wouldn’t help.

Sarah Beth wasn't even eating. She was making a picture of the *Mona Lisa* on the table with dry cornflakes. I think Mona winked at me. I was glad she didn't do anything strange enough to slow us down.

Finally, Mom drove us all over to Dinosaur Discovery.

We met Moose and Mouse in the parking lot. Their dad would give all of us a ride home later.

"We'd better hurry," I said. "The line's pretty long."

I started to run, but Libby grabbed my hand. "Are you sure this won't be scary?" she asked.

"I'm sure," I told her. I still wanted to run, but I couldn't drag Libby too fast. I reached the line just a second after Quentin Two.

I watched each person ahead of me buy a ticket and get a bobblehead. "Sweet!" I said when I saw Quentin's.

The triceratops was my favorite. Maybe he'd trade if I got a different dinosaur.

"I'm getting four tickets," I told the ticket guy. "We each get a bobblehead, right?"

The man shook his head. "Sorry. We just ran out."

"Ran out?" I said. That wasn't fair. The triceratops would have been mine if Libby hadn't slowed me down.

"At least they didn't run out of tickets," Sarah Beth said, giving me a pat on the shoulder. I was so disappointed.

After Moose and Mouse got their tickets, we all stepped inside.

Dinosaur Discovery was super scary.

But it was scary in a good way.

Libby clutched my hand harder, but I didn't see fear in her eyes. I saw wonder.

"You okay?" I whispered.

Libby nodded.

We walked right underneath a gigantic apatosaurus. I had a feeling if I looked in a mirror right now, my own face would be pretty much as wonder-struck as Libby's.

There were signs all around the room.

"Read it to me," Libby said.

"Scientists think dinosaurs might be related to birds," I read aloud.

As I said the word "birds," a tiny ripple of worry ran through my stomach. I'd read Libby a book about a blue*bird* last night. *Don't be silly,* I told myself. *There's nothing to worry about.*

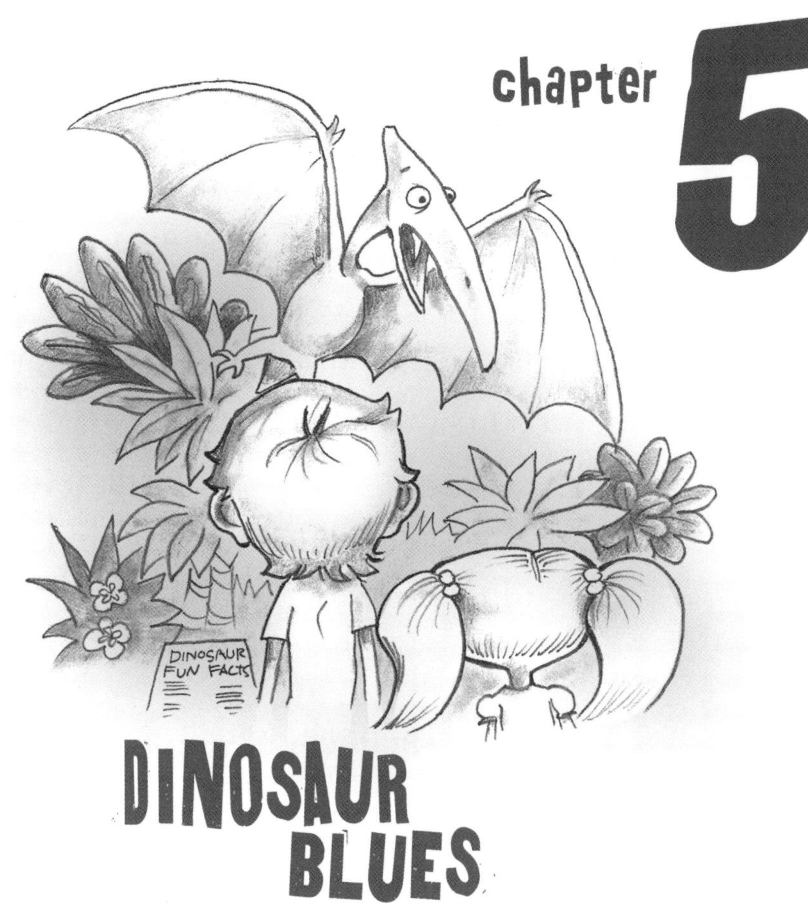

chapter 5

DINOSAUR BLUES

We walked to another sign.

"No one really knows what color dinosaurs were," I said, reading that sign aloud. "Some scientists believe they were green. Others feel they might have been blue, or red, or even striped."

The dinosaurs all around us were lots of different colors.

"Look, there's a blue one!" Libby said. "That's my favorite color."

Blue birds . . . blue dinosaurs . . . I didn't like the way this was going.

Libby ran across the exhibit hall and threw her arms around the left hind leg of a dinosaur. I followed her and read the name plate:

•AMIGOSAURUS•
RECENTLY DISCOVERED
AND NOT YET CLASSIFIED

"This one is my favorite," she said.

The amigosaurus moved its head and roared. If I looked carefully, I could see some gears inside its mouth, but I didn't want to look carefully.

I wanted to pretend all the dinosaurs were real, even though they were just robots that kept repeating the same series of motions. They couldn't really eat one another or walk like real dinosaurs.

"Libby, look over there!" I said. I wanted her to stop thinking about blue dinosaurs.

Next to the amigosaurus, we saw an amazing T. rex bend down and take a bite out of a fallen raptor. We watched for a while as the T. rex took the same bite over and over.

"Scared?" I asked Libby.

"No. He looks like Uncle Lucas when he eats watermelon at the family picnic," she said, giggling.

Derwin stuck his tongue out at the dinosaur. Then he turned around and stuck his butt out.

As I walked away, I heard a scream. I spun back just in time to see the T. rex chomping Derwin's butt.

"Help!" Derwin shouted as he rose high up in the air.

"Catch him, Mouse!" I shouted.

Mouse ran over with his hands out and caught Derwin just as the T. rex opened his mouth.

I was afraid we'd get kicked out. Luckily, the guards were busy chasing Quentin Two.

After we'd seen everything at least ten times, rescued Derwin from the T. rex two more times, and pulled Libby away from the amigosaurus five more times, Moose called his dad. Then we headed for the exit.

As we drove away, I caught a glimpse of something large and blue slipping out the rear entrance of Dinosaur Discovery.

I touched the coin in my pocket and then whispered to it, "Behave yourself."

chapter 6

CAN WE KEEP IT?

I didn't see anything else on the way home. Even so, I figured it might be a good idea for us not to hang around outside.

"Well, I have a report to write," Sarah Beth said as she headed inside. "Stay out of trouble."

"Let's all go inside," I said.

"No, let's play Wiffle ball," Derwin said. He grabbed a bat and ball from the garage.

"It's too windy," I said. I spotted something blue far down the street, heading our way. *Maybe it's just a big truck*, I thought.

"It's not windy," Moose said. He took the ball from Derwin. "Back up a little. I'll pitch to you."

I really wanted to get inside. I wondered whether I could use my Stranger power to *make* the wind blow. I had a quote book in my room. Mr. Sage, the owner of the New Curiosity Shop, had given it to me when I'd told him how my brother, Derwin, made my quotes, like **A PICTURE IS WORTH A THOUSAND WORDS**, come to life. Mr. Sage knew a lot about strangeness.

Moose tossed Derwin an easy pitch.

The ball sailed down the street. Everyone raced after it. I was close behind them, but then I stopped in my tracks. Something huge was thundering toward us.

It was definitely a dinosaur. Trucks don't run on two legs. And trucks aren't as tall as the trees.

"Wait!" I shouted. I could feel the ground

shaking beneath my feet.

Everyone froze — not because of my shout, but because they finally noticed the dinosaur, too.

The dinosaur grabbed the Wiffle ball in its mouth. Then it walked toward us and opened its jaws. I noticed there weren't gears inside anymore. The ball dropped out, landing at Derwin's feet.

"Maybe we should back away," I said. My brain told my feet to move, but I guess my feet were too busy staring. Even after all the strangeness the Silver Center had caused, this was the most amazing thing that had ever happened to me. But it was also the most dangerous. It was one thing to watch mechanical dinosaurs. It was another to have a real one on the loose, with no idea what it would do.

The dinosaur turned its head toward Libby. It opened its mouth wider. It had a whole lot of enormous teeth. The dinosaur's head dropped lower. A giant tongue came out. I grabbed the bat so I could try to protect my sister.

Before I could reach Libby, the dinosaur licked her.

The tongue was so big, it lifted her up on her toes. The dinosaur licked her again. Then it closed its mouth and sat back on its hind legs.

I ran over to her. "Are you okay?" I asked.

Libby wiped her face with her hand. "That was fun." She petted the dinosaur on the leg. "I'm going to call her Bluebird."

"Her?" I asked.

"Of course," Libby said.

"Bluebird is a stupid name for a dinosaur," Mouse said.

Bluebird swung her tail, giving Mouse a gentle nudge that knocked him halfway across the street.

"On second thought," Mouse said as he got back to his feet, "it's a great name."

She's big, but she doesn't seem to want to eat us, I thought.

"Come on, Bluebird," Libby said. "Let's go play. We can have a tea party. Then you can take a bath with my ponies." She headed for our house.

"Libby, you can't bring her inside," I said.

She stopped on the porch. "You're right." She pointed at the welcome mat and said, "Please wipe your feet first, Bluebird. That's the rule."

"No, Libby," I said. "She'll break the house!" I tried to think fast. "Go play in the backyard."

"Oh, all right," Libby said. She headed around to the back. Bluebird followed her. Derwin, Mouse, and Moose started to follow her, too, but I stopped them.

"What are we going to do?" I asked. *And what had the Silver Center done to me?* I wondered whether I had finally created a mess that was too big, and too strange, to fix.

chapter 7

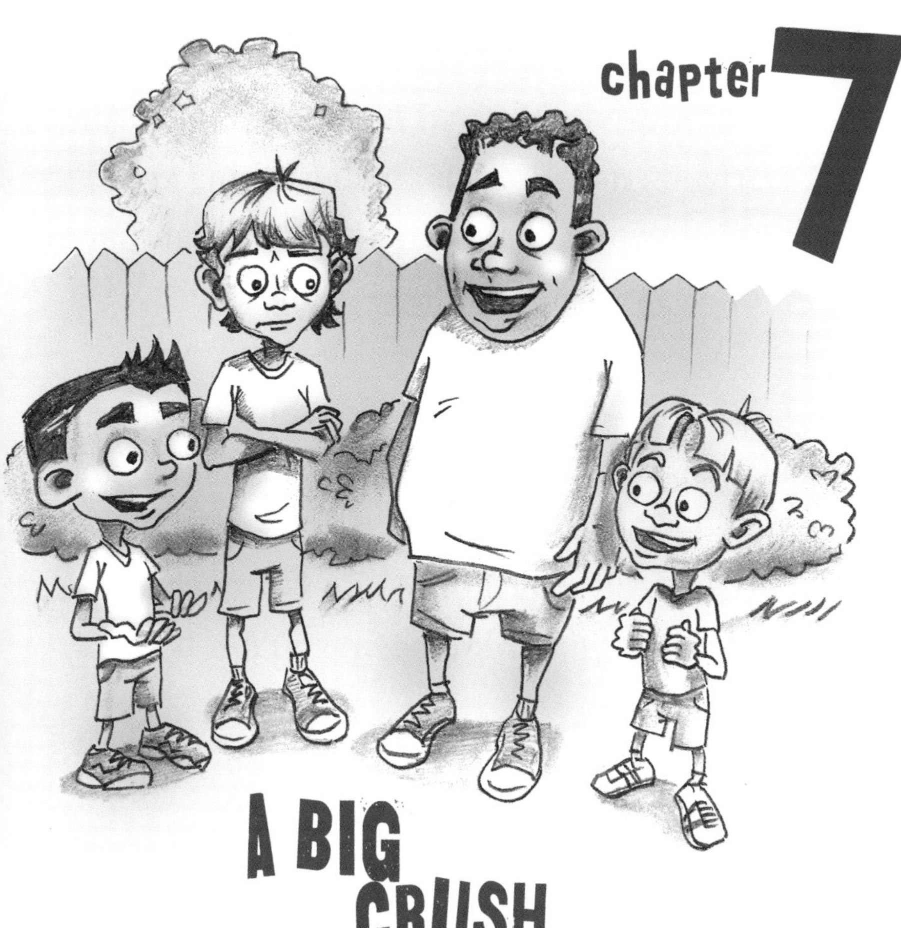

A BIG CRUSH

“What are you talking about?” Derwin asked. “We have our very own dinosaur now! How cool is that?”

“It’s not ours,” I said. “We could get in trouble for stealing it.”

"But we didn't steal it," Moose said. "And Derwin's right. This is the best thing *ever.*"

"It's nice having something around that's almost as strong as I am," Mouse said.

"Maybe even stronger," Derwin said.

"Definitely taller," Moose said.

Just then, Libby popped into sight and yelled, "Come see! Hurry!"

We raced after her. When we reached the backyard, Bluebird was lying on her belly.

"Oh, no! Is she sick?" Derwin asked.

"No," Libby said. "I taught her a trick. Watch." She turned toward the dinosaur and said, "Roll over."

Bluebird rolled over — right over Rex's doghouse.

Rex growled at Bluebird. She licked him. He shook himself, ran to the other side of the yard, and started digging a hole. I guess he wanted to bury Bluebird. He'd need a month to make a hole *that* big. I looked around for my cat, Willow, but didn't see her. Maybe she was hiding.

Libby grinned. "I'm going to teach Bluebird lots of tricks."

I looked at the remains of Rex's doghouse. I couldn't let my parents see it before I had a chance to fix it. I ran inside and dragged my tent up from the basement.

"Moose, give me a hand," I said. We set up the tent in front of the doghouse. Everyone else might not agree, but I knew I had to get Bluebird back where she belonged, and back to how she was. The people at Dinosaur Discovery expected her to be a robot, not a real dinosaur. And I had to figure all this out before Mom or Dad got home.

As Libby, Derwin, Moose, and Mouse started teaching Bluebird to crawl on her belly, I slipped away and headed for the New Curiosity Shop.

"Hello, Ed," Mr. Sage said when I ran in. "You seem upset."

"I'm fine," I said. "But I have a little problem." I told him about the dinosaur.

"You must get it back where it belongs," he said.

"But how?" I asked.

"It will follow your sister," he said. "Have her do it."

"But she wants to keep it," I said.

"I'm sure you'll think of something, Ed," he said.

"That's it?" I asked. "That's your advice?"

He shrugged. "The Stranger has to think for himself."

"I never asked for this job," I said.

"But you accepted it," he said. "And you're going to find an answer. I have faith in you."

"Thanks," I said.

As I pushed open the door, I noticed a sign:

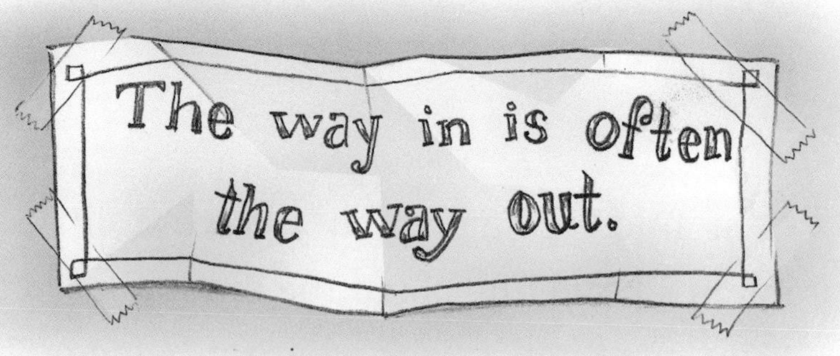

The way in is often
the way out.

If only dinosaurs were as easy to deal with as doors.

“I better find a way out,” I muttered. I rushed home. Mom would be there soon. I was running out of time.

When I got home, I noticed Mouse was lying on the back-porch roof.

“What happened?” I asked.

“I tried to arm-wrestle Bluebird,” he said. “She won.”

“No kidding,” I said.

As Mouse was climbing down, I heard Mom's car in the driveway. She was home. And we had a dinosaur in the backyard! Parents are nowhere near as calm about this sort of thing as kids are. I was pretty sure it was a good idea not to let Mom meet Bluebird. This mess was going to be a lot harder to deal with than anything else my Stranger power had ever caused. I'd already swept up after mice, pigs, and a pony . . .

I couldn't just sweep up a dinosaur.

I spun toward Libby and shouted, "Quick, Libby — tell Bluebird to hide!"

chapter 8

A FISHY PLAN

"Crawl, Bluebird," Libby said, pointing to the bushes at the back of our yard.

Bluebird flopped on her belly and crawled into the bushes. It was a good thing she was smaller than a T. rex. Even so, half of her tail was sticking out. I stood in front of it.

Everyone joined me. Just then, the back door opened.

"Oh, there you are," Mom said. "Did you have fun with the dinosaurs?"

"We still are," Mouse said.

I jabbed him with my elbow and said, "We still are talking about how great Dinosaur Discovery was."

"Why don't you come inside to have some lemonade?" Mom said.

"We can't!" I blurted out before anyone moved. Everyone loves Mom's lemonade.

"Why not?" Mom asked.

I looked around frantically. When I saw the tent, I said, "Because we're camping."

Mom smiled. "Well, enjoy your game. I have errands to run. I'll be back before dark." She walked off.

I slumped down, accidentally taking a seat on Bluebird's tail. She didn't seem to notice. "We have to get her back to Dinosaur Discovery," I whispered to Moose.

"Maybe you can lure Bluebird there with food," Moose said.

"Great idea," I said. "What do you think she eats?"

"Hopefully not us," Mouse said.

"I'll check online." Moose pulled out his phone and started searching. "Wow, I don't see much. I guess the amigosaurus is a really new dinosaur."

"Try Wimpypedia," Mouse said. "They have information about everything."

"My teacher told us Wimpypedia isn't very accurate," I said.

"It's better than nothing," Mouse said.

"Here it is," Moose said. "According to Wimpypedia, the amigosaurus loves fish."

"Are you sure?" I asked.

Moose held out the phone.

"We have some fish in the freezer," I said. "I'll go get them."

Moose pointed to Bluebird. "We'll need a lot more than a couple of frozen fish to get *her* to follow you."

There was only one thing to do. I went to my room to grab the quote book. Moose followed me, but Mouse went off to challenge Bluebird to an arm-wrestling rematch.

I found the section on fish quotes and started reading them to Moose:

**GIVE A MAN A FISH, HE EATS FOR A DAY.
TEACH A MAN TO FISH,
HE EATS FOR LIFE.**

I liked that, but I didn't see how it would help. I read another fish quote:

THAT'S A FINE KETTLE OF FISH.

I knew that one. Dad said it when things were really messed up. Whenever he said it, I could just picture a big kettle spilling over with fish.

"That one could work!" I said.

"We'd need a kettle," Moose said.

"A really big kettle," I said.

"Candy Castle!" we both shouted.

That was a store in town that made kettle corn, fudge, and other sweets. They had a huge kettle out front.

On the way down the hall, I spotted Sarah Beth in her room. "Hey, I know something that can help you with your report," I said.

She looked up and said, "No thanks. I have everything I need."

I shrugged and headed to the kitchen to grab a grocery bag. "Can you stay out back with Libby?" I asked Moose. "I'll need Mouse and Derwin with me for my plan to work."

"Sure," Moose said. "I know the perfect way to keep Bluebird busy."

When we reached the backyard, Moose threw the Wiffle ball. Bluebird ran after it, flattening our old sandbox. I added that to my list of things I'd have to fix.

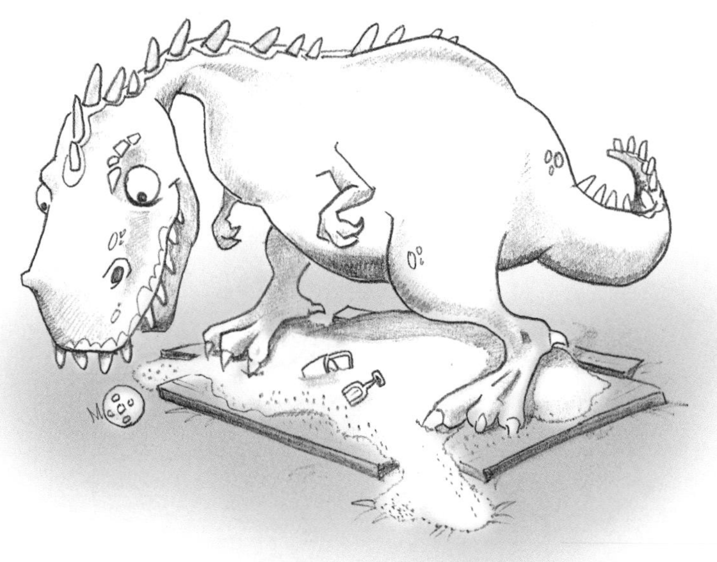

Mouse was on the back-porch roof again. I told him and Derwin that I needed their help. Mouse could do strange things I suggested, like lifting himself up in the air, even if they seemed impossible. And Derwin could make sayings come true. My power as the Stranger worked on both of them, but in different ways. There was a lot about the magic coin I still didn't understand.

Hoping I wasn't about to make things even worse, we headed for Candy Castle.

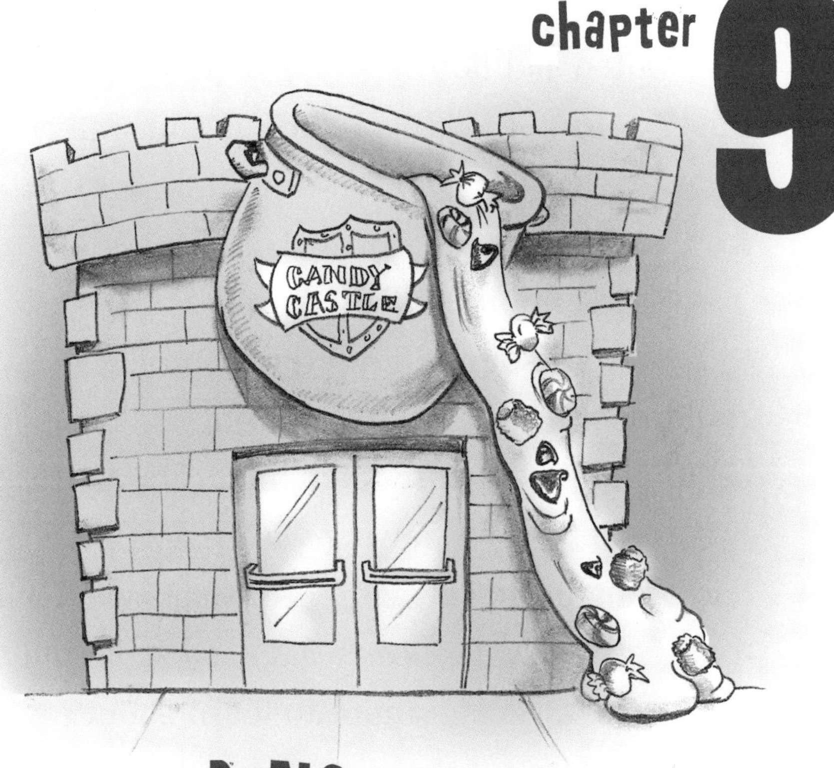

chapter 9

DINO BAIT

When we reached Candy Castle, I said **"THAT'S A FINE KETTLE OF FISH."**

"There aren't any fish in it," Mouse said.

"*Sshhhhhh,*" I hissed at him.

"The kettle's empty," Derwin said.

I waited, but nothing happened. "This will never work," I said as I turned and walked away. "What a mess. It's definitely **A FINE KETTLE OF FISH**."

"Whoa!" Mouse shouted.

I heard a sound like a thousand gigantic raindrops hitting a metal roof. I turned back, and my jaw dropped open. The kettle was suddenly overflowing with fish. Derwin had brought the saying to life. *Maybe quotes work better when I mean what I say.* It looked like there was even more to learn about my power.

I gave Mouse the bag and said, “Make a trail of fish from Dinosaur Discovery to our house. Go fast, but not as fast as possible.” If Mouse ran as fast as possible, things got really hot. One time, he ran so fast that he melted a box of chocolate bars! I wasn’t sure Bluebird would like overcooked fish.

Mouse filled the bag with fish and zoomed away. “Come on,” I said to Derwin. “Let’s hurry home.”

As we left, I heard Mouse behind me, whooshing back to the kettle for another load of fish.

On the way home, we ran into Quentin Three on his skateboard.

"Hey, Quentin! Want to trade one of those bobbleheads for a chance to see something amazing?" I asked.

"Where?" he asked.

"Behind my house," I said.

"Not if your cat's around," he said. "I'm terribly allergic. Remember?"

"Don't worry. Willow is hiding from Libby's new friend," I said. "Come on. You won't be sorry."

We reached the backyard just as Mouse was laying out the last of the fish, making a line that stretched all the way to Dinosaur Discovery.

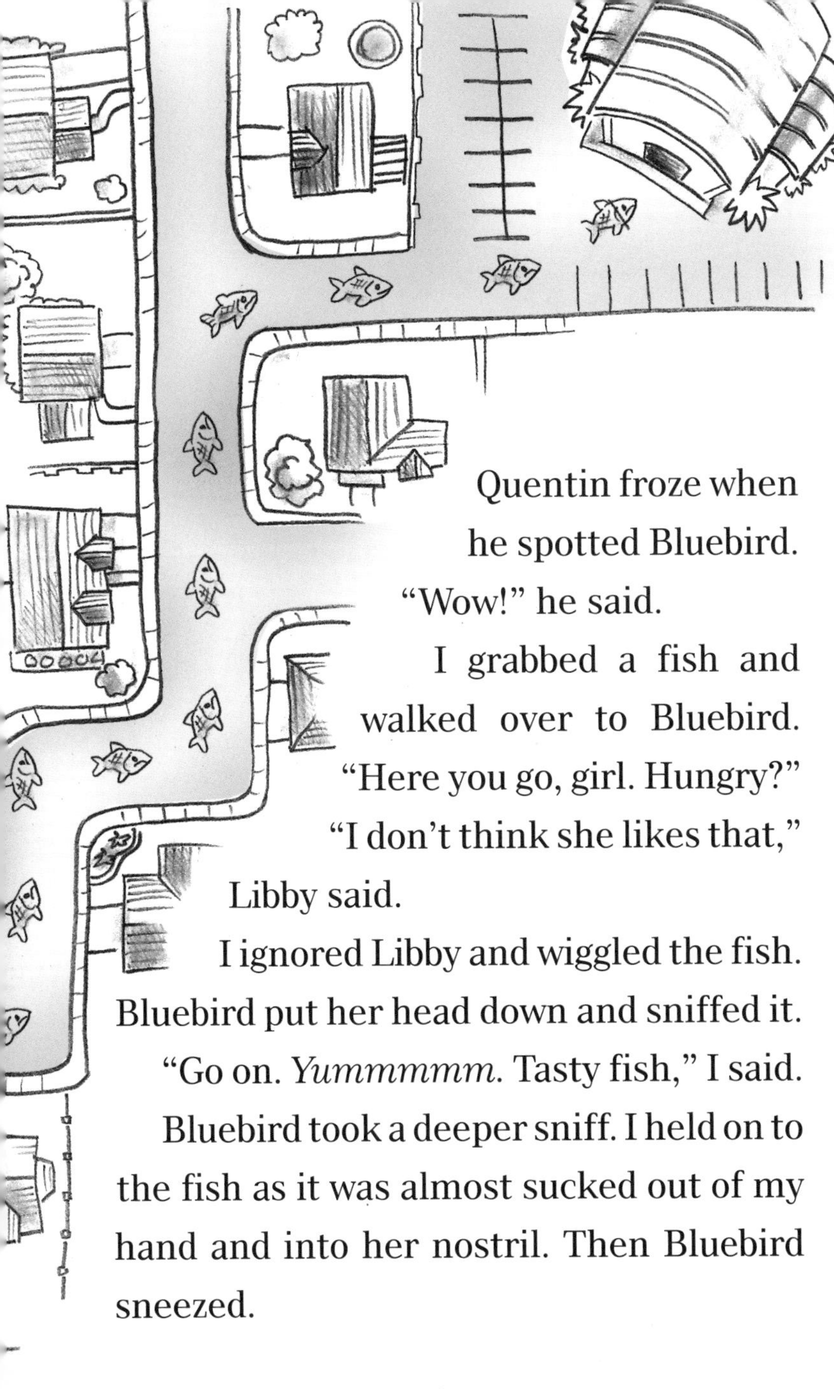

Quentin froze when he spotted Bluebird.

"Wow!" he said.

I grabbed a fish and walked over to Bluebird. "Here you go, girl. Hungry?"

"I don't think she likes that," Libby said.

I ignored Libby and wiggled the fish. Bluebird put her head down and sniffed it.

"Go on. *Yummmmm.* Tasty fish," I said.

Bluebird took a deeper sniff. I held on to the fish as it was almost sucked out of my hand and into her nostril. Then Bluebird sneezed.

ACHOOOOO!!!

There is really no way to describe what it feels like to be on the wrong side of a dinosaur's sneeze. The best I can do is compare it to having a giant bucket of warm glue thrown full force at your face.

"Here, Ed," Quentin said, tossing me a triceratops bobblehead. "That was definitely amazing."

I looked at Moose. "I thought you said she'd eat fish."

He shrugged. "I guess our teacher was right about Wimpypedia."

Things can't possibly get worse, I thought as dinosaur snot dripped down my shirt. That's when I heard the cats. Yes — cats. Lots of them. I guess they'd followed the trail of fish. Hundreds of cats were racing into our yard.

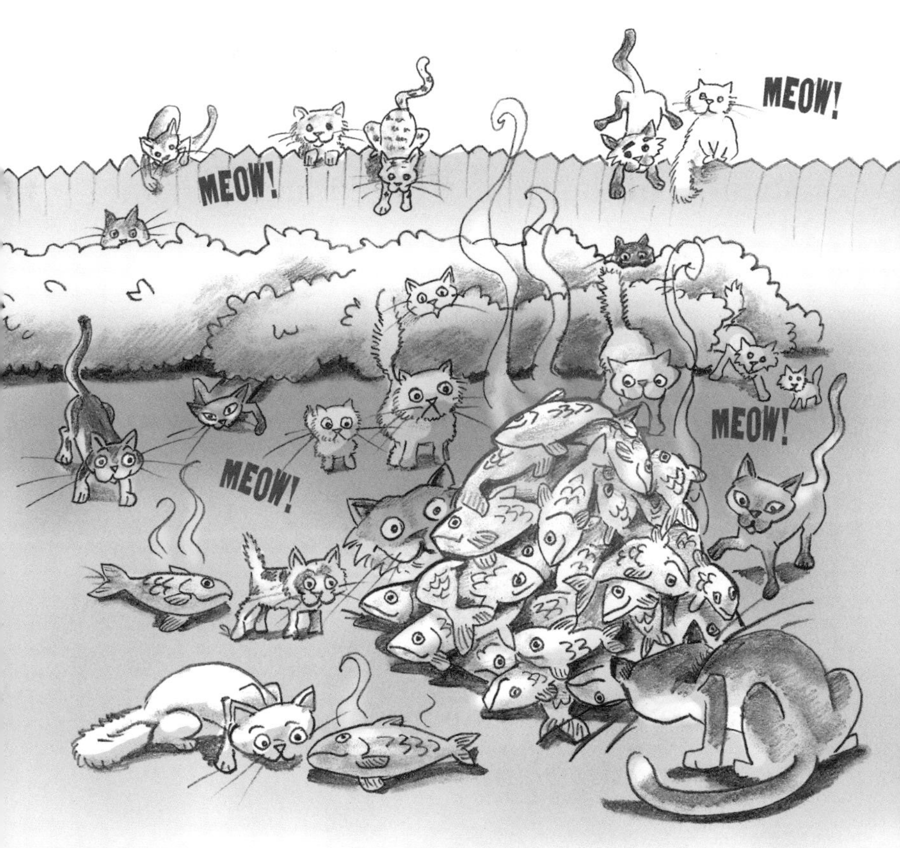

Quentin sneezed. He was a lot smaller than the dinosaur, but his sneezes weren't all that much less messy.

"Sorry," he said. "I'd better go."

As the cats filled up our yard, Bluebird screamed and leaped behind Libby, crushing the birdbath. I guess Bluebird was afraid of cats. Maybe she'd never seen one before.

"Go back where you came from!" Libby shouted at the cats. "Leave Bluebird alone!"

The cats dashed off. Libby's words echoed in my head: *Go back where you came from.* On top of that, I remembered the sign from the New Curiosity Shop:

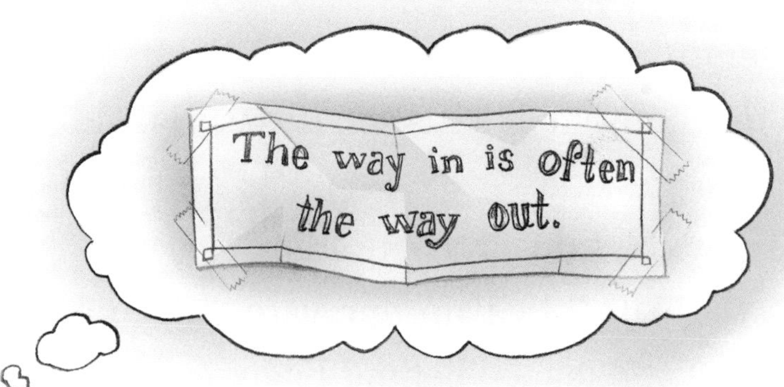

The way in is often
the way out.

"That's it!" I said, snapping my fingers. I knew what to do!

chapter 10

PICTURE THIS

"What now?" Moose asked. "Are you going to fill the yard with dogs?"

"How about giraffes?" Mouse asked.

"No. I have an idea that might actually work," I said. "If a book got us into this mess to begin with, maybe it can get us out, too."

I told Moose my plan. We left Libby, Derwin, and Mouse playing with Bluebird, and headed for the library. I wasn't worried about the backyard since there was nothing left to smash.

As Moose and I searched through the picture books, someone stepped up behind me. "Are you looking for a specific book?" she asked.

I turned toward the voice. It was the librarian, Ms. Oberdew.

"Sort of," I said. "I want a book that will help my little sister learn to put things back where they belong."

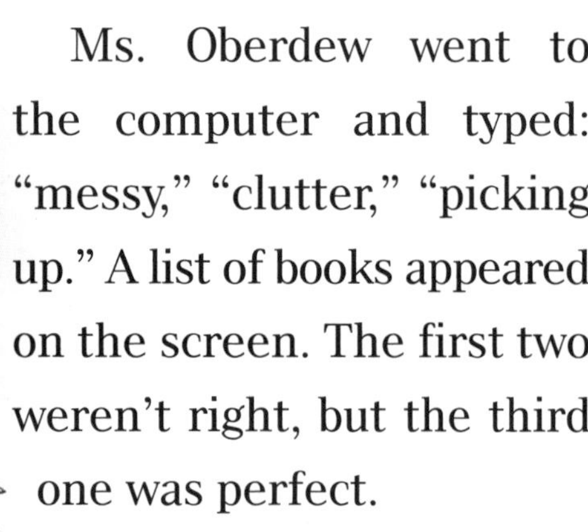

Ms. Oberdew went to the computer and typed: "messy," "clutter," "picking up." A list of books appeared on the screen. The first two weren't right, but the third one was perfect.

READ

"Can I get that one?" I asked, tapping the screen.

"Oh, dear," she said. "It's checked out. But it's due back by next Tuesday. Do you want to reserve it?"

"No, I really need it now," I said.

"Then why not write your own book?" she said. "That way, it will say exactly what you want."

"Can I do that?" I asked. I'd written stories in school, but I'd never written a book.

Ms. Oberdew pointed to another computer at the other end of the table. "We encourage young writers to create their own books. Give it a try."

Wow. This was something I'd never even thought about. If I could make any book I wanted and read it to Libby, and if what I read to her came true, the Silver Center gave me more power than I'd ever imagined. The thought excited me.

"Moose," I said, tapping him on the arm, "have you ever wanted to write a book?"

"All my life," he said.

It turned out Moose was a good writer, and I was a good artist. Together, we created a picture book and printed it out. The librarian helped us attach a cover.

"Very nice, boys," she said after we were finished.

"Thanks for the help," I said. Then we both ran back to my house.

chapter 11

STORY TIME

When we got back to my house, Bluebird was playing fetch with Libby and Derwin. Mouse was climbing down from the back-porch roof. The yard looked pretty torn up, and Rex was still digging. The hole was huge, but still nowhere near big enough to bury Bluebird.

Moose called his parents to ask if he and Mouse could sleep over at my house. He didn't want to miss anything.

Mom got home right after dark. We made Bluebird hide in the bushes again. Luckily, Mom just peeked out the door and didn't notice the crushed sandbox or birdbath. When Dad got home, he built a small campfire for us. Luckily, whenever Dad makes a fire, he gives it all of his attention.

After Dad left, I plopped down in front of the tent and told Libby, "It's time for us to read a story."

She sat down next to me. Moose, Mouse, and Derwin sat on my other side. I guess they realized this wasn't a normal story time. Bluebird put her head in our laps.

"This story is called *The Girl Who Put Everything Where It Belonged,*" I told Libby.

"That sounds silly," she said. But she didn't interrupt me when I read it to her.

"Good night, Bluebird," I said as I crawled into my sleeping bag. The dinosaur looked at me with sad eyes. Sometimes, it wasn't easy to do the right thing. Overhead, the moon shone down on us just like it had shone on the dinosaurs long ago.

"I hope this works," I said to Moose.

"Me, too," he said. "It's totally cool that we got to play with her. But you're right, Ed, Bluebird just doesn't belong here."

I just hope she belongs somewhere. . . .

chapter 12

GET BACK!

When I woke up, Libby was sitting next to Bluebird. I guess she hadn't done anything yet. But if my plan worked, Libby would put Bluebird back where she belonged today.

Libby wrapped her arms around Bluebird. "I love you, Bluebird," she said.

Bluebird started to glow, like she was filled with light bulbs. The air around her shimmered. Then it changed. All around her, like a movie was being shown, I could see a world of giant plants. A huge insect flew past. A warm gust of air washed over my face. I smelled strange fruits and flowers.

WHOOSH!

Bluebird started to get sucked back into her world. But Libby grabbed for her.

"Let go!" I shouted.

"No!" Libby yelled.

I grabbed Libby. I could feel myself getting pulled.

Hands gripped my shoulder. Moose had grabbed me. Then Mouse grabbed Moose. And Derwin grabbed Mouse. Rex grabbed ahold of Derwin. Derwin yipped as he got nipped in the butt, but he didn't let go. Willow dashed up to Rex and grabbed his tail in her teeth.

We all yanked.

Then Libby let go. And we all flew backward through the air. I braced for a hard landing, but I plopped down in something soft.

There was a flash of light as Bluebird whooshed back into the prehistoric jungle. As the image faded, I saw another dinosaur that looked just like Bluebird, but a lot bigger. That dinosaur ran up to Bluebird and licked her face.

I looked to my left, where Libby was sitting on the ground. Her arms were crossed and her eyes were filling with tears.

"You made me lose her," she said. I guess Libby figured out I could make her bring stories to life.

"I'm sorry," I said. "But Bluebird had to go where she *really* belonged."

She nodded and wiped away a tear. "I know, Ed."

I was about to get up when I realized why my landing had been so soft. Bluebird had left me a present. A big, stinky one. Everybody cracked up. But I didn't mind. I had a feeling it was Bluebird's way of thanking me.

Besides, I was getting pretty good at cleaning up all sorts of messes. When you live in a Looniverse of strangeness, you have to be ready to deal with anything. You even have to deal with friends who think everything is funny.

But, hey, I did say I'd do *anything* for that bobblehead. And if I can keep learning more about how to control my Stranger power, who knows what will happen next?

Check out the next LOONIVERSE book!

DAVID LUBAR loves writing weird and funny books, such as *Beware the Ninja Weenies: And Other Weird and Creepy Tales.* He likes dinosaurs, cats, and fish, though he rarely comes up with a way to get all three in the same place or on the same page. He hopes you enjoyed reading this Looniverse story as much as he enjoyed writing it. He lives in Nazareth, PA, with two real cats and several awesome unreal dinosaurs.

MATT LOVERIDGE loves drawing dinosaurs! In fact he loves it so much, that he sometimes becomes a Mattasaurus! This is a large, slow-moving, peaceful dinosaur. Mattasaurus eats many different kinds of foods including fruits, vegetables, and the occasional bacon cheeseburger. Mattasaurus lives in a small family group, which can be found in the mountain regions of Utah. He is known to communicate through a series of doodles and scratches. Mattasaurus can't stick around for long though—Matt Loveridge has too many crazy things left to draw in the Looniverse!